To Mary

w/ ♡

Dad

2010 AD.

Cloudwalker

Contemporary Native American Stories

Joel Monture

Illustrated by Carson Waterman

fulcrum kids

Golden, Colorado

For Joseph, Mary and Elijah with love from your father
(Konna:rohn'kwa)

Library of Congress Cataloging-in-Publication Data

Monture, Joel.
    Cloudwalker : contemporary Native American stories / Joel Monture ; illustrated by Carson Waterman.
        p.   cm.
    Contents: We have no word for art — The animals give themselves — Grandfather crosses over — Cloudwalker — Pow-wow — Water spirit.
    ISBN 1-55591-225-7 (hc)
    1. Indians of North America—Juvenile fiction. 2. Children's stories, American. 3. Short stories. [1. Indians of North America—Fiction.] I. Waterman, Carson, ill. II. Title.
PZ7.M7715C1   1996
[Fic]—dc20   95-42815
                                                                CIP
                                                                    AC
Printed in the United States of America

0 9 8 7 6 5 4 3 2 1

Fulcrum Publishing
350 Indiana Street, Suite 350
Golden, Colorado 80401-5093
(800) 992-2908

Contents

Introduction

As Native Americans move into the twenty-first century, we find that much is changing in our world. Yet sometimes it seems that nothing has changed regarding stereotypes. We are still asked by mainstream America if we live in tipis, eat buffalo and wear war bonnets; and the fact that Native people have VCRs and cellular telephones seems to surprise people. Even more strange is the notion that names like Colleen or Fred, or even Joel, seem somehow not to belong to Native Americans.

With the encroachment of technology, from computers to satellites, Native people of the Americas find themselves with a foot in two worlds—working as attorneys or artists during the week, and returning to traditional values, families and communities on weekends, or even integrating traditional thinking into the modern workplace.

There is a subtle perception that a Native American in a suit and tie or a lab coat, or perhaps standing behind a teacher's desk, has abandoned his or her heritage. But nothing can be farther from reality. Similarly, but in reverse, there is a widespread notion that all Native people—even if they were raised mainstream in Detroit—have within them a vast mystical knowledge and the ability to heal the world with ritual and ceremony. Both views are untruths. Further complicating issues is the concept by mainstream America of what an "Indian" should look like, which is usually based on Hollywood images. The Native people of the Southwest are very different from the people of James Bay, and the cultures are very different as well. But there are some universal ways among Native people that have nothing to do with occupations or physical appearances.

Thousands of years of knowledge about the natural and spiritual world form much of the basis of Native community, belief, behavior and experience. Some things don't change, despite the wearing of designer jeans or sneakers. Native ways are different, not just traditionally but also within the dynamics of family and community.

This collection of stories is for all children to celebrate life in its various facets from Native perspectives. These stories are about life and loss, creativity and destruction. They are from the point of view of Native children, who themselves are learning about their worlds, which seem to rush at greater speeds. If you tip up your ear and listen, you will hear the laughter of falling leaves, the rumble of thunder, the crying of birds. ... And it will sound like our children's voices.

Cloudwalker

Contemporary Native American Stories

Cloudwalker

Virgil Bill, a nine-year-old Mohawk boy from Six Nations
Indian Reserve, nestled along the banks of the Grand River in
Ontario, Canada, thought about his father as he worked in the
garden hoeing the corn, beans and squash—the traditional food
the Mohawks call the three sisters. The three sisters were also
called the "Great Sustainers," because they sustained life, making it possible for people to live. Many traditional people de-
pended on the three sisters during the winter months, but sometimes that was not enough.

So the men went away to work and to earn money, and they
would send it home to their families. Virgil was thinking of his own
father as he labored in the garden. Virgil's dad was far away working, walking in the clouds.

Virgil's dad, like so many Mohawks over the years, was a
high-steel worker. Sometimes the men were hired in crews to
build big suspension bridges, but most often they walked upon
long steel girders, keeping their balance as they constructed sky-
scrapers. Virgil had never seen a high-steel construction crew at
work, but he imagined they were like birds on high perches, with
their heads in the clouds.

When Virgil was finished working in the garden he ran to the big old wooden barn. Virgil wanted to be just as brave as his father. He had been practicing his balance by walking on a narrow board, pretending that he was high in the sky. Today he would really walk in the sky!

Swinging open the creaky barn door, Virgil ran to the ladder that led up to the loft where the hay for the horses was stored. Up he climbed until he stood on the edge of the loft, looking out at the big wooden beams that stretched across the open barn. Above him he saw the pigeons flapping through the cracks of light that shined through the barn roof. Virgil made up his mind to be brave as he placed one foot on a beam that was about ten feet above the floor of the barn. He told himself to pretend that it was just a board on the grass.

Slowly, he put his other foot on the beam and stood there in the sky, right up among the pigeons. He concentrated—feeling as brave as his father—wishing he would grow up faster so he could join the construction crews. Slowly, holding out his arms for balance and looking straight ahead, he inched along the beam until he was in the middle of the open barn. He didn't dare look down, because he was afraid he would become dizzy and fall.

Suddenly a loud voice rang out, "Virgil, be careful!"

His mother stood in the open door of the barn, her hands on her hips and a worried look on her face.

Virgil slowly kneeled down and crawled along the beam back to the loft, and then he climbed down the ladder. He hung his head down as he walked up to his mother, feeling foolish for getting caught pretending to be a high-steel worker.

His mother lifted up his chin. "Don't be in such a hurry," she chided. "Your turn to walk on beams will come soon enough!"

Later that day, sitting in a tidy kitchen in their small, clapboard log house eating a dinner of sweet corn and butter beans, slices of ham and tomatoes from grandmother's garden, the telephone rang. When Virgil's mother answered it, her face lit up with a big smile. When she hung up the phone, she exclaimed, "We're going to New York City to see your father! Some of the men can't come home for Harvest Celebration this weekend, so we are going to visit *them!*"

Virgil felt like he was about to burst with such exciting news. He had never been to a construction site, and he couldn't wait for the weekend to arrive.

The night before their trip, Virgil had a hard time falling asleep. All he could do was think about seeing his dad; maybe some uncles or an older cousin or two would be there also! When he finally fell asleep, he dreamed about being a bird and flying in the clouds beside the steel workers high in the air.

In the morning, Virgil ate his breakfast quickly. Then he sat in the car while his mother loaded traditional foods—corn soup and fry bread—and other bags into the trunk. Virgil had never traveled far, and the thought of seeing new places was very special. Finally they left, joining a caravan of four other cars, and Virgil watched as they passed rolling pastures with cows grazing, fields of grapevines ripening in the sun and corn turning brown with the approach of autumn.

They drove for several hours, crossing the Rainbow Bridge beside Niagara Falls. Virgil had never seen anything so wonderful as the falls, with millions of gallons of water rushing over the great horseshoe-shaped rim of the cliffs. "It was us, the Mohawk people, who helped build this bridge," Virgil's mother told him. After a while, Virgil began to feel tired, and he leaned against the seat with his pillow and slept.

Later, all the cars stopped and everyone worked to make lunch—bologna sandwiches and commodity cheese from the government. Then Virgil played in a green grass field with his cousins, kicking a ball until it was time to drive again.

When it was almost dark, Virgil began to doze again. He felt his mother nudge him. Looking up, Virgil covered his mouth in surprise. Ahead of them was New York City, reaching into the sky and lit up like a million stars had fallen to earth!

Driving through the streets of New York was exciting and scary. There were so many cars and people, and the buildings seemed so tall Virgil could not see the sky! They parked near an apartment where the ironworkers lived together. It was a sight to see all the people carrying bags and bowls of food and jugs of strawberry drink, like a circus parade. Virgil held his mother's sleeve when they went into the old brick building, and followed along as they climbed stair after stair, before traveling down a hallway. Altogether there were twenty people, and when one of the elders knocked on the door, there was a great sound of voices greeting. Virgil looked up among all the people trying to find his father! Someone lifted him up from behind and spun him around, and Virgil saw his dad's big happy smile!

"Welcome to New York, Virgil," said his dad and Virgil wrapped his arms around his father's neck and squeezed tightly. Inside the sparsely furnished apartment, Virgil watched as the women brought out tablecloths and began to set out food as everyone talked and laughed. Virgil sat right beside his dad when an elder called for quiet and began to address everyone, reminding them to be of good minds and offering a thanksgiving for all the gifts of life the Creator bestowed on the people. He talked for a very long time, and when he was finished everyone began to eat. Later, someone got out a little water drum and some rattles, and the men who were singers sat on chairs in a line in the middle of the room and sang social songs. Everyone danced. When it got late, Virgil's mother arranged a corner for him with a blanket and his pillow, and he fell fast asleep.

In the morning when he woke up, the men were all gone.

"They leave early for work," explained his mother, "but after breakfast we'll go visit the construction site."

Back in the car, Virgil's mother pointed out a structure, like a toothpick skeleton, that rose high in the sky among all the tall buildings. "That's where your father is," she said with a smile. As they drove closer, Virgil saw that it was constructed of huge iron I-beams held together with thousands of iron rivets. High up top tiny figures as small as ants were working.

Virgil's mother parked the car and told him to wait while she went to the site office. A short time later Virgil saw her walking beside his dad, and he jumped out of the car and ran up to his dad.

"How'd you like to go up top?" asked his dad.

"You bet!"

Virgil walked between his dad and his mom, and they entered a big iron cage, Virgil's dad closed the door and pushed a green button on a gray metal box, and with a great lurch the cage began to rise slowly up the side of the building. They were no walls or windows; and Virgil could see right through each story. Turning back, he could see out over the city of New York, and just like in his dream they were rising higher than the pigeons!

Virgil felt a little scared. He asked his dad, "Do you ever get scared going up so high?"

"Everybody gets a little scared," laughed his dad. "But that helps you remember to be extra careful and look out for your buddies. We work together to be safe."

Somehow that made Virgil feel better about being afraid when he walked on the barn beam, and he was happy his dad was careful.

When they arrived on the top level, Virgil's dad opened the elevator door, and they all stepped out onto a broad floor of thick wood planks littered with piles of I-beams and construction tools. A big crane on the far side of the building was swinging a girder into place while a crew of men guided and set it into position. There was a lot of noise and yelling of orders, and the air smelled like hot oil. A strong breeze whipped across the work platform.

All of a sudden Virgil was surrounded by men in hard hats, their sleeves rolled up exposing dirty arms. He looked up into their sooty faces and began to smile. Here was his Uncle Wilbur and his Uncle Lester. There were cousins Earl, Harvey and George and many other men he didn't know. All together they began to sing "Happy Birthday." Virgil suddenly remembered what day it was. In all the excitement he had forgotten his own birthday!

His dad reached toward Uncle Wilbur, and Wilbur brought a bright orange hard hat out from behind his back—the same kind the steelworkers wore to protect their heads—and there was the name VIRGIL printed across the front! Virgil's mother gave him a gentle push, smiling at him, and he swelled up with pride when his dad placed the hard hat on his head. The men all gave a cheer and patted Virgil's back.

Then Virgil's dad took him all around the construction site, explaining everything that was happening. "I'm the foreman," he said. "Sort of like your lacrosse coach. It's all about teamwork, and we work hard, just like playing a game hard."

Virgil's dad pointed out the rodmen who tie steel rods in place for concrete, and the connectors who raise beams into place and set the steel. There were all kinds of jobs and each was important.

"Look there!" said Virgil, tipping his chin toward a long beam. A man walking along the beam suddenly stopped in the middle and did a handstand. A man at the other end of the beam hooted.

"There was a great connector who always did that once the connection was made and the steel was solid," laughed his dad.

"Really? Who was it?"

"Me!" said his Dad.

Virgil's mother spoke up. "I didn't know that. Virgil don't you dare try that in the barn!"

"The barn?" asked Virgil's dad.

"I caught him walking the beams in the barn!"

Virgil's dad laughed again, "It's in his blood!"

Then Virgil's dad let him walk along a beam—not one connected in place—but one that was stacked in the center of the work area. It was about four feet off the deck, and Virgil knew, after seeing his father's look of pride, that someday he too would be a cloudwalker!

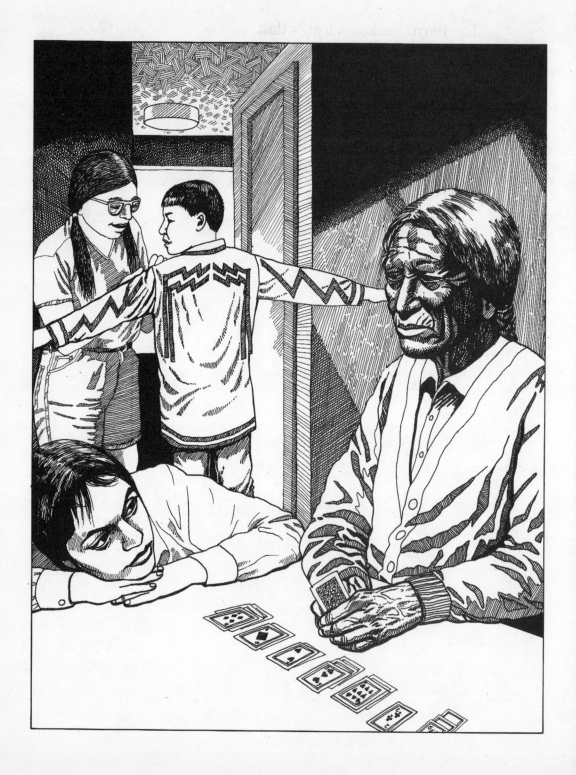

Grandfather Crosses Over

In the rugged high country of northwestern New Mexico, the leaves on the aspen trees were turning bright yellow and fluttering in the wind, a sure sign that winter was coming to the people of the Jicarilla Apache nation.

After getting off the school bus, twelve-year-old Doreen Vigil ran beside the road, tugging along her younger brother, seven-year-old Hector. She loved the crisp smell of autumn, when everything was changing and the leaves were dying and falling to earth. Grandfather had explained that autumn was part of the cycle of life, when plants and leaves return to nourish and feed the earth. Then winter comes—a time of sleeping. Spring was full of new life, new leaves, the whole earth blooming again so that it would grow all through summer!

But these were the cool colorful days Doreen loved the most. She didn't even mind that her little brother was so slow beside her as they turned into the dirt driveway that led to the small white frame house, nestled among the sweet-smelling piñon pines and scrubby cedars. She lived with Hector; her mother, Alice; her Auntie Carla and Grandfather Charlie Vigil.

Both Mother and Auntie worked at the tribal office in the town of Dulce, so it was always Grandfather who first greeted them when they arrived home from school.

Today she could see smoke rising from the tin stove pipe on the roof, and the thought of the crackling fire in the old iron stove warmed her before she even entered the house. When Doreen and Hector came inside the house, it was toasty warm. They tossed their coats beside the door.

Grandfather, standing at the far end of the living room in the open kitchen area, cleared his throat, "Hey there! Hang up your coats!" Doreen and Hector obediently hung their coats on low hooks on the wall beside the door. Hector jumped on the couch to watch the television in the corner of the living room.

Grandfather was a short old man. He was wearing a worn button-up sweater; his long gray hair was pulled back in a single braid that Auntie made for him every morning. His face was full of brown wrinkles, and he smiled all the time. Doreen came over and asked what he was doing at the kitchen counter.

"Benny Wounded shot an elk yesterday, and he shared the meat with us. He's a good friend." Grandfather was cutting up meat and wrapping it in wax paper to put in the freezer. "Hey, you got any homework?"

Doreen pouted. "It's no fair. Hector never has homework."

Grandfather put down the package of elk meat. "You know that's not really true. Homework is about learning on your own. Sort of like climbing trees or chasing rabbits. It's about figuring things out in life." He tapped her on the head. "What's up there, girl?"

Doreen had been asked that question a million times, but still she answered. "Brains, Grandfather."

"And what are they for, Doreen?"

"To think with, Grandfather."

"You know," Grandfather said, "Coyote, the Trickster, says that our heads are round so our thoughts can change direction!"

Doreen got the homework out of her little knapsack and sat at the kitchen table, working on math problems while Grandfather watched cartoons with Hector.

When she finished her homework, Doreen sat on the other side of Grandfather, feeling his gentle arm around her shoulders.

After a while, Grandfather said, "Hector, you go out now and feed the horse, not too much corn. Doreen, you start boiling up some stew meat. Momma and Auntie will be home soon."

"What are you gonna do, Grandfather?" asked Doreen.

"I'm gonna rest here a little while. I feel tired today."

It was getting dark earlier. Doreen, filling a big pot with water at the kitchen sink, could see little Hector in the shadows of the little corral out back, feeding an old roan horse some corn from both his open hands, laughing to feel the horse's soft muzzle tickling his palms. Then he tossed some hay in a feeder trough and filled the water tank from a hose. Doreen thought, "For a little kid he does alright." She really did like Hector, even if he didn't have homework. She looked over at Grandfather and smiled. He was still sitting on the couch sleeping, with his chin down. He snored just like a big old bear!

When Mother and Auntie came home it was just about dark, and Doreen had already set the table. Mother gave Hector a big hug and tapped Grandfather on the shoulder, "Dad, wake up. It's almost supper time."

Grandfather looked up and blinked. "Doreen's cooking elk," he said.

Mother's round face beamed with a big smile. "Doreen, it smells real good in here! You have a good stove!" Auntie went to the stove and tasted the broth in the kettle, then winked at Doreen.

Auntie said, "We'll just put in some salt, and some carrots and potatoes!"

After dinner Grandfather and Auntie sat at the kitchen table. Grandfather played solitaire with an old deck of cards, while Auntie worked making beaded earrings, picking up beads on her thin needle from a leather pad. Mother measured Hector for a new ribbon shirt she was making for his birthday. Doreen sat at the table, resting her chin on her arms, listening as Grandfather talked.

"My grandmother was Chiricahua," he said, "and she was with Geronimo when the Army was trying to catch them. The Army tried for years but couldn't catch him. Grandmother said it was because every time the Army got close, the men turned into cactus and the women turned into rocks. The people had powers, just like all the rest of the beings in the real world … ."

Doreen listened to Grandfather tell stories all evening until it was time for bed.

The next morning, Doreen was sitting at her desk in school, looking out the window as the wind blew leaves like small tornadoes. The teacher came and tapped her on the head. Doreen turned and said quickly, "Brains?" She giggled to herself thinking about Grandfather.

Then the door to the classroom opened, and Doreen was puzzled to see her mother standing there, holding Hector's hand.

Mother's face was not smiling, and when the teacher came over to her, Mother leaned in close and whispered to the teacher.

The teacher said, "Doreen, you may go home with your mother."

In the car, Doreen asked her mother what was wrong.

Mother turned and slowly said, "Your Grandfather is gone. He crossed over to the other side this morning. Benny Wounded found him sleeping on the couch and called Auntie and me. Grandfather didn't wake up. He was very old."

Doreen leaned her head against the car window and stared at the passing road. Everything seemed to rush by so fast! All of a sudden she wished her head was square, so that all the thoughts in her mind would stop changing directions and be clear to her!

When they got home, there were many cars parked around the house. Inside there were also many people—neighbors and relatives who were there to honor Grandfather. Doreen, so accustomed to having Grandfather there, felt that the house was empty. Many people had brought over food and were talking together in low tones. Doreen felt very alone, and she ran out the back door. She ran so fast, past Grandfather's horse in the corral, through the piñons and pines until she was far up a hillside among the aspens.

She sat on a rock and looked all around at the falling leaves. The cold wind was bringing the leaves down, back to earth where they had come from, and they lay on the ground, silent and still. Doreen began to cry. Then she got up and started to kick the leaves!

"I hate autumn!" she yelled out loud in the aspen grove. "Why do leaves have to die? Why does anything have to die!"

Then she sat on the rock and thought about her Grandfather. After a while she heard her mother calling her name. She got up and slowly walked back to the house.

Her mother gave her a long hug when they met by the corral and said, "It's okay to feel angry. But there are some things we cannot change."

Mother tipped her chin toward the corral; Doreen followed her gaze.

"See that old horse of Grandpa's? She knows, too, and she's sad."

Doreen watched the horse standing, hanging her head low, just the way Doreen felt.

"How does she know that Grandfather died?" asked Doreen.

"Because the air is filled with so many thoughts about him, and they were friends. She knows that something has changed. She just knows it in different ways than you or I."

Then Doreen left her mother's side and went into the corral. She slowly came up to the old mare, and they looked at each other. Doreen put her arm around the mare's neck and whispered in the horse's ear, "Tell Grandfather I miss him."

The mare snorted, and Doreen smiled.

In the days that followed there were so many activities, and Doreen kept thinking of Grandfather as the ceremonies to release his spirit took place. The leaves continued to fall, and the season kept changing.

Doreen went back to school. Winter arrived, then spring, and before long another year had passed. When the aspens started to change color again Hector was complaining about homework. Doreen thought about how Grandfather had always been there when they came home from school, starting supper and making Doreen sit at the kitchen table to do her homework.

"I don't know what to do!" whined Hector, staring at his homework. Doreen came and glanced at the math problem.

"It's so simple!" she said.

"I don't get it," said Hector.

Doreen tapped his head. "What's up there, boy?"

"Brains?" said Hector.

"What are they for?" asked Doreen.

"To think with?" said Hector looking at the math problem again. "I got it!"

Then Doreen smiled and went back to peeling potatoes.

She could see the old mare through the kitchen window and said under her breath, "Grandfather, Hector's okay … for a kid!"

We Have No Word for Art

A cool breeze rippled the short brown buffalo grass across the rolling plains near Crow Agency, Montana. Chester Whitebull, a member of the Apsaalooke nation, thought he could smell a fresh spring rain coming. The air was crisp, like the bite of winter, even though it was already April. Chester pulled up his jacket collar as he ran after his friends, trailing them up a winding coulee that led away from the Little Big Horn River. Chester was a curious boy, always eager to go exploring. Today he and his friends had been trying to catch a little prairie dog, but it was too fast for the boys.

"Wait up, you guys!" Chester called, digging his cowboy boots into the soft earth. Melting snows had left the gullies muddy, and it was hard for ten-year-old Chester to keep up with the bigger boys. "Travis … Ronnie … wait up!"

The steep walls of the coulee were high above Chester's head. When he came around a curve he saw his friends standing still. They were staring at a bank of earth that had washed out from the melting snows. Travis Redbird was thirteen and big for his age, with long black hair and a round face. Ronnie Frechette was twelve, with short brown hair and a long lean frame. Chester slipped up through the mud until he reached them. "What is it?"

Travis tipped up his chin to point at the wall of bare earth.

"Wow!" said Chester looking at the open bank of earth. He had never seen anything so beautiful. The earth revealed layer upon layer of colored clays like a rainbow. It curved along the bank, and some of the layers sparkled with chips of mica. Overhead the rain clouds had made the sky gray, but the colored layers of earth were bright.

Chester scrambled over the washout to reach the rainbow of colors.

"What are you doing?" asked Ronnie.

Chester looked back. "I think it's earth paint, like the old-timers used!"

"So?" asked Travis"

"I want to take some," said Chester, "to show my mother." Chester began to dig at a vein of earth that was green like copper. "You guys help me!"

A sudden rumble of thunder shook the sky.

Travis and Ronnie looked up at the clouds. "Come on," said Ronnie. "There's a storm coming!"

Chester didn't care about the storm. He scooped a handful of green earth, then wondered where to put it. He shrugged and filled the back pocket of his jeans. The wind began to blow harder. Chester squinted over his shoulder. "Well?"

Travis grunted "Kids!" Then he scrambled up to the bank with Ronnie following. The three boys began digging at the different colors and loading their pockets.

A few drops of rain started falling. Chester was excited, having fun as he dug in the bank. He didn't notice the rain until it really began to shower. Then a really big clap of thunder rattled the clouds and a streak of lightning lit up the western sky. Chester looked up. "I guess we have enough. Let's go!"

Chester jumped off the bank and ran up the wash, climbing a grassy knoll to the road on top. Travis and Ronnie scrambled after him. The three ran along the road until they came to several small, low, wood-frame houses. Old cars rested in the grass beside many of the houses. Behind Chester's house was a framework of tall, narrow pine poles, which was used for a tipi during the summer.

Shivering as he burst into the house, Travis and Ronnie close behind, Chester called out, "Mom! Look at this!"

Chester began to empty one of his pockets of earth onto the kitchen table when his mother, Arlene, appeared, buttoning up her sweater.

"What are you doing?" she asked. Travis and Ronnie took a step backward.

"It's earth paint!" said Chester, excitedly. "We found it in a washout."

"Hold on there," said Chester's mother, getting a newspaper to spread on the table. "Let's see what you have."

Chester motioned to Travis and Ronnie, and the three boys stood around the newspaper emptying the different colored earth from their pockets into separate piles on the newspaper. Mrs. Whitebull looked on, smiling gently.

On the newspaper, the earth didn't look nearly so bright as it did outside under the gray sky. But there were very different colors—a rusty red-brown, a blue-black, a coppery green, a mustard yellow, a chalky white—and shades in between.

"How do you know about earth paint, Chester?" asked his mother.

"I heard Grandma talk about it once," he answered.

"Is this really paint?" asked Travis.

"I told you it was," smiled Chester.

"Maybe it's not all paint," said Chester's mother, "but some of it might be. We should get Grandma. She'll know."

Pulling a brown canvas coat over her shoulders to protect her from the rain, Mrs. Whitebull went to Grandma's two-room house just fifty yards away.

Chester looked at his two friends. "I told you it was paint!"
Travis said, "I think crayons and markers are easier."
Ronnie said, "And faster!"
"You'll see," said Chester. "My grandma knows a lot! She's very old."

A few minutes later the door opened, and Mrs. Whitebull helped her mother enter the house. Grandma, a small woman with white hair pulled back in long braids, carried a bundle wrapped in an old shawl. She had dressed in a traditional outfit as though this was a special occasion. Chester's mother carried another bundle.

"Hi, Grandma," said Chester.

Grandma came over to the table. "You been out in the dirt?" she asked. She squinted at the piles of earth on the table. She gave two big claps, then covered her smile with one hand. She reached down and touched some of the piles of earth. "This one's just mud! Throw it back." Then she pointed at four colors—black, red, green and yellow. "Paint," she said.

Chester swelled inside. "See? I told you!"

Everyone was quiet and polite as Grandma opened her bundle, untying the thongs around the old shawl wrapping. Inside was a cylinder made of rawhide with designs painted on it. The colors were very faded and worn. "This was my grandmother's paint set," she said, slowly opening the top and reaching inside. "These were all the things she used to paint her designs."

"Was she an artist?" asked Chester.

"Oh, we have no word for art," said Grandma. "But I guess if you put it that way, at one time everyone was an artist. Everything was made beautiful to look at."

Grandma carefully laid out the objects from inside the rawhide case—small beaded pouches containing powdered pigment, different lengths of peeled willow sticks used to measure lines, small porous bones for spreading the paint inside the designs, a few old clamshells with little bits of dried paint in them and an awl for scoring designs on leather or rawhide.

Mother unrolled the second bundle—a very old buffalo robe—and carefully laid it on the floor, fur side down. The skin side was covered with colorful pictographic paintings of warriors and horses. Chester and his friends marveled at the wonderful scenes on the robe.

"This old robe belonged to your great-grandfather," said Grandma. "And these pictures are his stories from the old days. Here you can see him charging into a great battle." Grandma traced the outline of her father on the old painted robe.

Chester's mother said, "A robe was not just used for a blanket, but like clothing to wrap up in. Sometimes there was beadwork or porcupine quill embroidery on them in bright colors, but most often they were painted. Women's robes and men's robes had different designs."

Chester and his friends admired the robe, studying the scenes of Chester's great-grandfather capturing enemy horses. Chester chuckled, "The ponies are red and blue and green!"

"Whoever said ponies have to be just brown and black? Why, they can come in all colors!" said Grandma clapping her hands and smiling. "Even yellow and purple!"

Travis and Ronnie looked at Chester. Travis said, "Maybe we could use some of that earth paint to make ponies?"

"It's a lot of work to do it the old way," said Grandma, "but I could show you."

"Yes!" said all three boys in unison.

Chester's mother said, "I guess I'll call your mothers and tell them you're staying for supper."

Grandma sat down in a chair at the kitchen table. "Get some paper and a pencil, and I'll show you how to draw."

Later as the boys were drawing, Mother boiled hot dogs and cooked up a big pot of macaroni and cheese. They gobbled up their supper as they practiced drawing ponies, comparing their pictures and laughing all the time!

After supper Grandma showed the boys how the old paints were mixed with glue made from hide scrapings, but she said they could even use Elmer's glue or mucilage. She carefully ground up some pigment into a fine powder and mixed it with watery glue in a clamshell. Then she used the porous edge of a bone brush to draw lines on a scrap of leather. "That's how it's done!" she said.

After a while Travis's mother and sister arrived. Then Ronnie's older brother came in. Before long the small kitchen was filled with people listening to Grandmother teach the boys. Everybody praised the boys when they held up their pictures.

"It used to be that only men painted real pictures and women painted only the geometric designs," said Grandmother. "But now anyone can paint whatever they like."

"When I grow up," announced Chester, "I will be an artist!"

"You already are!" said Grandmother. "Everybody is an artist when they create something."

Travis held up his drawing of an elk. "What do you think, Grandma Whitebull?"

Grandmother squinted. "It's a nice picture. But it doesn't matter what I think. If that's what's inside you and you are happy, then that's all that matters."

Ronnie said, "I like *my* drawing. It makes me feel good." It was a picture of a man on a pony chasing a buffalo.

With so many people crowding the small house, Chester's mother cooked more food. Everyone ate and laughed while the boys copied the images from the old buffalo robe. Suddenly the front door blew open, and a man appeared, soaked from the heavy rain.

"What's this ... a party?" he said. It was Chester's dad, and he had a big grin on his face. He brushed back a wet lock of hair as he greeted the family and visitors. He gave his wife a hug, saying,

"Arlene, the plane bounced us all the way into Billings! What a storm! But I'm glad to be home." Chester's dad had just returned from a conference in Washington.

"Grandma is showing the boys how to paint the old way," said Arlene Whitebull. "And it turned into a party."

Chester waved a picture at his father. "Dad, look at my drawing!"

Jimmy Whitebull came close to the table where the boys were working and looked at the picture. "If you had a pickup truck you could really chase that buffalo," he laughed.

Chester frowned. "Dad, this is the *old* way!"

Jimmy chuckled with the boys but then was serious, speaking very softly, "Remember always the life that came before you. Grandma gave you a gift tonight ... and one day you will give the gift to others."

Chester thought for a moment. "Dad, I know Grandma understands a lot, but I didn't think she was cool. She doesn't talk a lot, and she hates music. But now I think she's cool in her own way! Do you think Grandma can teach us other things too?"

Chester's dad tipped his chin toward the old woman, sitting in a soft chair in the living room and said, "Ask Grandma."

The boy left the kitchen table and went to his Grandma. "Grandma, do you know other things?"

"I might," she said smiling.

Then Chester leaned down gave her a hug and said, "I'll try real hard to learn."

Water Spirit

Louis DesChamp suddenly rolled off the log he was sitting on. He was laughing so hard his stomach began to ache, and tears rolled down his brown cheeks. His father, Rene, had just put the old wood and canvas canoe in the lake by the short dock. When Rene stepped in, the bottom broke, and he fell right through the canoe. He stood up to his waist in water, holding a paddle, with a surprised look on his face.

It was springtime in Maniwaki, Quebec, a land of forests, lakes and rivers which had been home to the Cree people for countless generations. It was also home to the majestic moose, loon, beaver, raven and eagle. The rivers and lakes were full of trout, salmon and bass, and it was a great thrill to go fishing after the spring thaws melted the ice on the lakes. Today, Louis was eager to go fishing, but seeing his father fall through the canoe was so funny.

"Hey, Dad," he called, regaining his voice, "catch any fish yet?"

Rene smiled and placed the paddle on the dock. "Help me get out of here."

Louis ran down and pulled on his dad's arm while Rene twisted out of the hole and climbed to the dock. "I hoped we'd get one more year out of that beat-up canoe, but I guess it's not even worth fixing now." Rene, with his short black hair and graying temples, was soaking wet. "Let's go in for a while, dry off, and think about this problem," he suggested.

They walked up a narrow path through the woods to a large log cabin in a clearing. It was a tight, warm house with a wide porch across the front under the second-story roof. Louis's mother, Margaret, sat at a table on the porch, sorting through porcupine quills that had been dyed bright colors—green, red, blue and yellow. Beside her were rolls of thin birchbark and a basket of tools, from scissors to needles and thread. She was making little birchbark boxes with bright quill designs, which she sold in Ottawa.

She clapped a hand over her mouth to hide a wide pretty smile, then said, "What happened to you?"

"I wish you had seen it, Mom," said Louis. "Dad fell through the canoe! I'm gonna get the catalogs and look for a new one." Then he raced into the house, letting the screen door slap shut behind him.

"Hey, I didn't say anything about buying a new canoe!" called out his father.

Louis reappeared behind the screen door. "How can we go fishing without a boat?" asked Louis. "We have to buy a canoe. Maybe aluminum or fiberglass, but not some old canvas boat! I have the sporting goods catalogs in my room."

"We'll take a look," Rene agreed.

Louis raced through the house, passing his younger sister, Marie, who was coloring with crayons on the floor in the living room. "We're getting a new canoe!" he called out, jumping up the stairs to his bedroom. He rummaged around in a dresser drawer for the catalogs that had bows and hiking boots and camp stoves ... and canoes!

Then he rushed downstairs toward the porch, eager to pick out a new canoe. The aluminum ones were shiny, but the fiberglass ones were bright colors, almost like his mom's porcupine quills. It would be so hard to pick out a color—red or green or blue or yellow.

"I got the books!" he said, spreading them out on his mother's worktable. A short time later Rene came out in dry clothing, and pulled up a folding chair. "Let's take a look," he said.

Louis thumbed through the catalogs until he came to two pages full of different canoes and prices. "I like that one a lot!" he said, pointing to a sleek red fiberglass model. "It comes in different sizes and colors, too. Some of them are twenty feet long," he said, reading the descriptions. "Boy, a twenty-foot red canoe would be great!" He looked up at his dad for approval.

Rene had a funny sparkle in his eyes. "How about that one?" he asked, pointing to the page.

Louis looked closely. The picture illustrated a white fiber-glass canoe with black streaks. It was called the "Birchbark Scout, Model 200," supposedly an imitation Indian canoe. "Dad, no way! It's so phony!"

"Why? What's wrong with it?"

"Birchbark canoes don't look like that. The white bark on the outside of the trees is supposed to be turned around. The brown inside bark is on the outside of a canoe, just like Mom's baskets and boxes."

"I guess they don't know what they're doing, eh?" asked Rene.

"Even I know more than they do, and I'm only twelve!" Louis wrinkled his nose.

"Brown is sort of like red, and I bet someone could make a twenty-foot birchbark canoe," said Louis's mother, who had been listening with a quiet smile.

Louis looked puzzled. He asked, "There are no real bark ca-noes in catalogs?"

"Of course not," said his father. "But we might take a drive this afternoon. What do you think, Margaret?"

"I think it would be a fine idea," she answered.

After a hearty lunch of sausages and boiled potatoes, Louis found himself riding in the family's jeep along a paved highway.

They turned onto a narrow gravel road. Louis's Dad was driving with Mom up front, while in the backseat Louis and his sister read books together in between watching the scenery. Marie loved it when Louis read to her, and she giggled when he made faces like the pictures of the animals.

After almost two hours of travel, they finally arrived at a small Algonquin settlement. Rene leaned out of the open car window to ask two boys carrying fishing rods, "Where is Jonas today?"

They nodded in the direction of the lake, and Rene drove a short way, parking the car near several old barns and a cabin. An old man with snowy white hair came around the corner of the barn as Rene got out of the car. Grandpa Jonas, as folks called him, squinted then grinned a big toothless smile, "*Bonjour!* Hello, Rene!" he called out.

Louis watched as his father gave the old man a strong handshake, then handed him a gift of tobacco and some chocolate bars. "Kids, Margaret, come and meet Jonas."

When Louis got out he was welcomed by Jonas, who took his hand also. His shake was very gentle when he squeezed Louis's hand, the way the old-timers did it.

"Louis, Jonas and my dad were best friends as boys. Jonas is a canoe-maker. He makes them the right way!"

Looking around the yard near the barns, Louis saw piles of wood shavings and strips of wood, big rolls of birch bark and slabs of cedar wood leaning in the shade of the barn. Just past the yard the lake glistened blue in the sunlight and reflected the billowy white clouds that drifted overhead. "This is a very interesting place," thought Louis.

"Jonas, you got any canoes around here?" asked Rene, winking then at Louis.

"Sure, I got some, not very big though. Come on down to the lake. I'll show you."

Louis followed close to Jonas as his family trailed behind, and when they reached the lake he saw three beautiful trim canoes resting on the stony beach. Louis ran up close to examine the workmanship, from the etched designs in the bark along the gunwales to the even spruce root stitching. His dad came beside him and said, "Maybe you want to try one out?"

Jonas leaned over and grasped the sides of the canoe, then deftly rolled it up onto his knees. Then balancing it, flipped the canoe until it rested on his shoulders. He carried it down to the water's edge and rolled it over with a splash into the lake. The canoe bobbed high on the surface of the water, and Jonas handed Louis a paddle.

"Go out. See how she handles."

Louis placed the paddle across the gunwales like his dad had taught him and maintained his balance by stepping right into the center of the canoe, kneeling with his legs spread wide for balance. Jonas gave the canoe a shove, and it glided silently onto the lake.

This wasn't like the old canvas canoe, thought Louis, dipping his paddle with short smooth strokes. This was a fast canoe! It rocked more from side to side because it didn't have a keel. But Louis didn't tip it over. He knew how to keep his weight lowered in the boat and keep balanced by bending with his hips. When he looked back he saw his family on the shore, waving. He spun the canoe around with several hard J-strokes, then paddled straight for shore.

"No," called Jonas. "Don't run up on the beach. Turn and come alongside."

Louis cruised in slowly and Rene grabbed the bow, helping him to step out onto the beach. "Dad, I really like this canoe!"

"You mean you don't want the red fiberglass one or the Birchbark Scout, Model 200, from the catalog?"

"Are you crazy? This is a real canoe! Not like those bogus ones! No, I think we should buy this one!"

Rene smiled, "This one isn't for sale. And it's too small for all of us."

"Those other ones look alright," said Louis. He wanted one of Jonas's canoes so much.

"I don't think those ones are for sale either. Jonas made them for other people. One of them is going to a museum in Ottawa."

"Then what are we to do now?" asked Louis, feeling let down.

Jonas spoke up, "Lots of work to do here. Maybe you can stay with me, help me make canoes this summer. Then you can have one. Your dad says it's okay for you to learn about canoes. Maybe we can go fishing."

"Until summer we can borrow Uncle Claude's canoe," said Rene, patting Louis on the back.

Louis thought he would burst! This was even more exciting than he had dreamed. "Oh yes, I think that's a great idea. I'll work really hard, Jonas!"

As soon as school ended in June, Louis arrived to spend the summer with Jonas. In the traditional way, he referred to Jonas as Uncle, a term of friendship and respect. And Jonas sure made him work hard! Louis learned how to use a crooked knife, an old tool for shaving soft cedar wood ribs and planking used to line the bark hulls of the canoe; and he learned how to dig and pull up long pieces of spruce roots from the sandy soil, splitting them to sew the birchbark.

Sometimes they got up very early in the morning and paddled across the lake while the mist swirled on the surface of the water, hearing the whistling songs of the loons as they searched for canoe-making materials—straight cedar trees and tall thick birches. Louis enjoyed working in the forest with Jonas, because the old man often paused to point out a bird or describe a certain animal sound. Jonas also told Louis about the different plants where they worked, how some were used for medicine, some for tea, some for food by the old-timers.

One time Louis asked, "How come my Dad doesn't know all this stuff?"

Jonas replied, "Oh he knows lots of this stuff, but did you ever ask him to tell you? The whole lake is full of fish, but people always think the big ones are on the other side! Sometimes you don't have to go very far to get what you want."

During the remainder of the summer, Louis became very good at stitching the bark hulls of the canoe. He even learned how to seal the seams where water would come in by covering them with pine pitch mixed with ground-up charcoal. The last step in finishing the canoes was to incise or scrape designs into the bark, which was Louis's favorite part.

By August, Louis had helped make six canoes, and one of them was for his family. It was a long canoe, with upturned ends and floral designs incised on the prows. It was big enough for his whole family to ride in, even the dog.

But the most special part of his summer was not just knowing how to make and repair birchbark canoes, it was that he and Jonas had become friends. For the rest of his life he would remember the lessons learned. When Louis and his dad went fishing together, Louis would always think of old Jonas, even years after he had passed away. When it was time for Louis to finally leave, Jonas gave him an old crooked knife with a moose antler handle. Louis reached in his pocket and gave Jonas a small beaver carved from cedar that he had made as a special gift. The old man nodded and shook the boy's hand, but this time the handshake was a little bit firmer.

Gliding silently at dawn through the lily pads the following autumn, passing ducks and loons, listening to the sounds of the natural world, Louis felt as if he were at the center of the universe with all the water spirits around him. He had learned so much living with Jonas for a summer, and in some ways Louis had changed. He still thought fiberglass canoes were okay, but a real birchbark one was better!

The Animals Give Themselves

"*E*lizabethhh!"

Betty Talon shifted restlessly on a pile of pillows and turned to her best friend in junior high school, Debra. "I hate it when she calls me *Elizabeth*! It always means I have to set the table or vacuum or do something stupid!"

"I know!" said Debra. "Just turn up the music and pretend you can't hear!"

Betty turned up the stereo and the two girls laughed, shuffling through magazines. Betty pointed to a picture of a girl wearing expensive clothing with lace ruffles. "Like everyone dresses like that at school. It's so phony!"

Betty, round-faced with short black hair, and Debra, blue-eyed and freckled, were both twelve years old and lived in Fairbanks, Alaska. Together they shared homework and videos and gossip while watching TV in Betty's bedroom in the small apartment. Betty was Koyukon, an Alaska Native nation, and Debra was Anglo, originally from Anchorage.

"Elizabeth!"

Betty flinched, hunching up her shoulders. "She sounds serious!" "Are you in trouble for something?" asked Debra frowning.

But before Betty could answer the door flew open, and Betty's mother was standing there. "I've been calling you!"

"Gee, Mom, the music was kinda loud … I didn't hear you."

"The music got louder after I first called," said Betty's mother. "I think you heard me," she said with a crooked smile.

"No, really Mrs. Talon. We didn't hear anything after you called," blurted out Debra.

Mrs. Talon smiled knowingly. "It's alright. I just wanted to tell you, Betty, that we're going home for potlatch."

"What's a potlatch?" asked Debra.

"It's a feast," said Betty. "People cook food and give away blankets. It's really silly. Do I have to go?" she asked. "Mom, maybe you could go and I could sleep over with Debbie?"

"No, it's our obligation. We are flying out tomorrow morning," said Betty's mother.

Debra perked up her ears. " You're so lucky to fly, Betty! I've never been on a plane. "

"It's so boring," said Betty. "You just sit in a seat and do nothing."

The next morning Betty found herself on a narrow seat in a small plane beside her mother, her overnight bag stuffed beneath her. "I really *hate* this," complained Betty. "Why couldn't I stay with Debbie for the weekend?"

As the little plane bounced along the runway and lifted into the sky, Betty felt her stomach jumping up and down. She felt excited as she watched the land shrink away. After a while, the earth looked like a quilt of rivers and snow. Looking down, it was as if the land was painted with an artist's brush—all smooth and blended—but the sun in the sky glinted off the water so far below, like silver ribbons crisscrossing the earth. Betty tried to see the roads and the towns, and she thought it was funny to see everything so small.

When the plane glided down with a thump on the runway, Betty was beginning to wonder if the potlatch might be fun after all. She would see her Uncle Vincent and Aunt Molly, and visit with her cousins. But most important was that her Dad, who was often away for months working with the tribe on natural resource issues, would be at the potlatch. If Betty lived in the small village she would see him more, but now Betty's mom worked in Fairbanks with a Native college fund program. Even though she missed her best friend, Debra, Betty was beginning to think that this weekend might be a great time!

Uncle Vincent met them at the airport. Betty and her mom climbed into the front seat of his old International pickup truck. Uncle Vincent had a thick accent and a missing tooth in the corner of his broad smile. "How you folks been doing there in Fairbanks?" he asked as the truck rumbled down a snowy road. Uncle Vincent, a hunter and a trapper, didn't travel very far from the village, except on his snow machine into the deep bush country.

"We've been alright," said Norma, Betty's mom. Norma was excited to see her husband, too, and share good food with family and friends.

They drove for almost an hour. Betty thought the land was a frozen wilderness, but to her mother it was the place she had grown up. She pointed out the ravens and the wildlife along the road.

Suddenly Uncle Vincent braked the truck and looked intently into the bush along the road. Norma watched, too, but Betty could see nothing. The bush was a tangle of saplings and scrubby bushes, and even with the snow on the ground it seemed like a dark place.

"What is it?" asked Betty.

Norma said, "Hush." Betty's mom pointed her chin toward the bush, and Betty looked closely, seeing a brown form moving very slowly. Gradually, Betty recognized it as a moose—a female, which is called a cow—whose breath made frosty puffs in the winter air.

Uncle Vincent quickly reached behind them for a rifle that was in a rack in the rear window of the truck, and he slowly opened the door, stepping out.

Betty looked at her mother. "He isn't going to shoot the moose?"

Before Norma could answer there was a loud crack from the rifle, followed by a short-lived crashing through the forest. Then silence.

Norma slid out of the truck and stood beside Vincent. Betty watched them talk in soft tones, then Norma said, "Come on, Betty we have a moose!"

Betty got out of the truck and whispered to her mother, "This is so gross! I hate it! Why can't we just go?" But Norma put her finger to her lips as a sign to be quiet.

There was a strange kind of quiet in the air, no wind. Everything was very still. Betty thought it was all spooky and she felt uncomfortable. But when Uncle Vincent and her mother left the road and hiked into the woods Betty followed, not wanting to be alone. The snow was not very deep, only up to their knees, but it was a struggle for Betty to keep up.

About 25 yards into the woods they came upon the moose lying on her side in the snow.

"Good shot, Vincent," said Norma.

Betty looked at the moose and saw steam rising in the cold air. "That's the biggest animal I ever saw!" said Betty.

"Oh, this is a small one. Maybe two years old," said Vincent.

"Mooses sure are funny looking … or do you call them meeces?"

Vincent and Norma both turned to look at Betty.

"I was only joking!" she said, casting her eyes down at the snow.

A gentle breeze picked up and a shiver ran through Betty, who pulled up the hood on her coat. She watched as Uncle Vincent leaned over and touched different parts of the dead moose, praying quietly. Betty looked up and saw some small birds land on bare branches, watching the scene below, their feathers fluffed up so they looked like little fuzzy brown balls with sparkling dark eyes and tiny beaks. Uncle Vincent continued to pray, offering a blessing to the spirits and a thanksgiving for the use of the animal.

Then he stood up and said, "Betty, run up to the truck and bring back the knives and saw under the seat."

Betty trudged through the snow, feeling confused. This was supposed to be a fun weekend vacation, a potlatch. Now here they were in the middle of the wilderness with a dead moose. It wasn't exactly bad, but it wasn't the kind of good time she expected. The dead moose made her feel kind of strange. She was used to shopping with her mother at the grocery store in Fairbanks, where all the food was wrapped up in nice, clean packages. She wondered how you would fit a moose in the microwave.

Reaching the truck, Betty fished under the seat and found two big knives in sheaths and a bow saw. She muttered under her breath, "This is so gross!"

Then she returned to the space in the clearing where her mother and Uncle were waiting.

Uncle Vincent and Norma both took off their coats. It was freezing, but Norma didn't seem cold. Without a pause she took one of the knives from Betty.

"Mom?" asked Betty.

"What? You didn't know that I'm an old moose skinner from way back?"

Betty was so surprised to see her mother working right beside Uncle Vincent. Norma began to explain. "I used to help my brothers all the time. My mother and I took care of the hides, and we smoked the skins for moccasins and mittens. When you were born and began teething, I used to give you a moose rib to chew on to help your baby teeth break out. You were weaned on moose!" she finished with a laugh.

"No way!" Betty protested.

Vincent laughed as he worked on the moose. "That's why you were so fat! You had real food!"

"I was not fat!" said Betty, feeling the center of attention.

Vincent and Norma looked up. "You were so chubby," said Vincent, "that you looked like a little meat pie!" Then they laughed.

"Come here," said Betty's mom. "Help us."

As they worked late into the afternoon Betty thought it was so strange to see her mother processing the moose. Betty was used to seeing her mother working in an office, wearing dresses and nice shoes and maybe T-shirts on the weekend … but not in the middle of a snowy bush skinning a moose. What else didn't she know about her mother?

Uncle Vincent worked fast. Before long Betty and her mother were carrying parts of the moose up to the back of the truck. "Just like when I was young," said Norma as they lifted a hindquarter of meat onto the bed of the truck. "Back then we had sleds and dogs. Now we use snowmobiles most of the time." After a while Betty was feeling hot, and she took off her coat.

When they were ready to leave, Betty noticed that the woods didn't seem still or quiet anymore. Birds were flitting in the trees, ravens were circling high in the sky, and a cold wind was blowing as they bundled up and started the heater in the truck.

As they drove along the snow-packed road, Betty thought to herself. This land was harsh, but somehow her mother was a part of it because she knew things. Once she looked back through the window to see the meat and the rolled-up moose hide in the back of the truck. As they cruised into the small village of tiny houses with smoking chimney pipes, Betty saw that there were no supermarkets, video stores or malls. This was the place her mother had been raised, and Betty suddenly felt as though she didn't know very much. It was one thing to listen to stories but very different to experience them.

The village was just a row of clapboard houses and sheds, with a few side streets. There were lots of dogs tied up by the houses, and snowmobiles parked under covers of canvas. Every so often Betty saw a moose skin stretched in a big wooden frame.

Uncle Vincent parked by a small house at the far end of the village, and they huffed up to the door, their breath steamy white as the sun set in the western sky, all yellow and purple. Betty followed into the house. It felt like a hot furnace from the rumbling woodstove. There were so many people, and Betty didn't remember any of them, but they seemed to know her. Betty was only a baby when she left, and her relatives rubbed her cheeks in welcome. She smiled as she felt all their hugs. Then, out of the crowd came her dad, David Talon. He picked her up, "Bettyboop!"

"Dad! Don't call me that!" she said, but she was still smiling. And she gave him a big hug. "We killed a moose for potlatch!" Betty didn't know where her words came from, but she somehow sensed the importance of this gathering of relations. Betty felt warm when her dad gave her mother a special hug, saying, "I sure missed you!"

"You got a moose?" asked Betty's dad. "You've been busy I'll bet." He sniffed her and added with a laugh, "You smell like a moose! Peee-U!"

That night Betty slept on the floor with blankets and a sleeping bag. She was so tired from working in the woods with the moose. She dreamed that the moose was talking to her, saying, "I give myself to you, so your people can eat and live." When she woke up, she thought her dream was real.

Betty found her mother having a cup of coffee with Uncle Vincent near the woodstove. Betty pulled her mother away.

Norma went alone with Betty to a quiet corner.

"Mom, I had a dream. The moose was there, and she told me it was like a gift to us. I don't understand."

Betty's mother held the warm cup of coffee in her hands and explained, "No matter how far we travel from home, when we return this is still our land. The place we come from. This is a place of people, ravens, moose and so many other beings, from the bears to the eagles. Long before there were TVs or trucks, we were here, and we supported each other. The Raven doesn't take more than it needs, and the people don't either. This is the balance of our world. Your moose visited you to let you know that it was alright. She gave up herself to feed your relations, because we paid respect to her nation. And from that you are learning to be respectful."

"I don't think I know anything!" said Betty feeling confused.

"You know hunters who have no respect get no meat. That's the same way around the world. All the spirits are talking. And they know who are the good people and who are the bad. You watch, here, how all this meat will be shared. Everyone will be fed from your moose. That's life."

"You mean, like the old saying `what goes around comes around'?" asked Betty.

Norma smiled. "See you can learn something even from a moose … or your mother!"

Just then Betty's dad came up. "Are you having a private conversation?"

Norma looked up and smiled, "Betty dreamed about the moose."

"Oh, I see," said Betty's dad. "Would feel better if I told you Aunt Esther makes moccasins? She'll make you a pair from your moose."

Betty beamed. "Really?"

"Maybe we should all talk more about our ways so we don't forget them," said Betty's dad.

"You're always gone," said Betty.

"Well, that could change," said her dad, his eyes twinkling. "I just happened to be transferred … to Fairbanks."

Norma jumped up and put her arms around him. "That's wonderful, David!"

"I guess I won't need the shortwave radio anymore to keep in touch," laughed Betty's dad. "But I'll still have to fly around the world."

"Do you have the radio here?" asked Betty. "Can we call my friend Debbie?"

Later, Betty's dad set up the radio and patched a call to Fairbanks. Betty held the microphone and talked to her friend, Debbie. All of Betty's family were standing around smiling. "Deb, we killed a moose!"

"Oh, that's so gross!" said Debbie.

"No it wasn't. We are going to have our potlatch feast tomorrow! I helped. It was really cool!"

"It sounds really weird."

"No, Debbie, it was okay. We said a prayer. It was about respect, you know?"

"Are you gonna come back?" asked Debra.

"I'm coming home … I miss you. Want me to bring home my moose?"

"You're so gross!!!"

"You're so bogus!!!"

Then both girls laughed, and Betty's dad turned off the radio.

The next day, Betty enjoyed the potlatch ceremony in the big room of the community hall. There was so much food. Elder members of the village stood up to make speeches about the unity of the people. Blessings were made in thanks for the natural world. Prayers were offered to the spirits, and everyone ate. All the people cooked big pots of stew and fried bread. Betty felt stuffed. "I never ate so much in my life. My moose was delicious!" Betty said to her mother afterward.

When Betty flew back to Fairbanks in the airplane she looked down at the landscape and saw her mother's village like little dots on the snowy earth.

Back home in her apartment, Betty was so happy to see her friend Debra. "Look what I brought you! A pair of moccasins. My auntie made them!"

Debra said, "I wish I could go to a potlatch!"

"Maybe next year, I'll ask my mom if you can come. But if we shoot a moose you have to help!"

Powwow

Homer John slowly waded back and forth in a shallow creek that ran into the Deer Fork River south of Stroud, Oklahoma. He leaned over, his hands held like horse blinders on either side of his eyes, as he stared into the clear water watching minnows scoot around the slippery rocks. "You're still in schools!" he laughed at the fish. Then he made a quick scoop with an open jar, catching half a dozen minnows. When he held them up the sunlight shined right through them and he could see their little bones. He was happy to be on vacation, and he was going to play all summer long!

It was not only the lush green hills or the sweet smell of hay in the humid summer air that thrilled Homer, it was almost powwow time. Soon the Sac and Fox fairgrounds would be filled with dancers and singers and booths selling buffalo burgers and Indian tacos!

Even more exciting, though, Homer's older brother, Lester, was coming home in time for powwow after being gone for almost two months to army basic training! Homer couldn't wait to show Lester all the new fancy dance steps he had learned. "This was going to be the best summer ever," thought Homer as he climbed up from the creek and pulled on his socks and sneakers.

Homer pedaled his bicycle along State Road 377 for almost a mile before turning onto a narrow dirt road lined with willow trees. He passed several small wooden frame houses. The Fasthorse family had a big old tractor tire lying in the front yard filled with bright orange marigold blossoms. Mrs. Fasthorse was pruning them, and she waved with a big smile on her face as Homer flew by on his bicycle.

Homer skidded into the driveway of his house, dropped his bike in the bare earth yard and ran up the wooden porch. He pulled open a crooked screen door and it banged shut behind him.

"Auntie!" he yelled. "I brought you something!"

Aunt Jeannie was sitting at the kitchen table doing beadwork on a pair of small moccasins. She was chubby woman with a broad moon face and brown hair pulled back with a brightly beaded barrette. "What have you got?" she asked as Homer twisted the jelly jar out of his pocket.

"Little fish," he said standing the jar on the table.

Auntie looked at the jar. "Let me see, yesterday it was Indian tea, and the day before it was Mrs. Fasthorse's flowers. I think you are bribing me to finish your moccasins sooner!" she said with a grin.

"Oh, no," said Homer. "I just thought you would like some fishes!" Homer looked at his moccasins, wishing they were done so he could practice dancing in them in the yard. All he had now were old worn-out ones handed down from cousin James. "I wouldn't bribe you Auntie."

But she smiled, and her eyes sparkled as if she could read his mind.

"You take a sharp knife and poke some holes in the lid so they can breathe," said Auntie. "Then tomorrow you take them back to their own place. We'll watch them swim around tonight."

Later in the day Uncle Lloyd came home from work on the highway crew. He was dark from the tar asphalt they were putting on the roads. Homer watched him stand at the kitchen sink, rolling his sleeves past his elbows. He scrubbed his hands and arms and leaned his face down to make it soapy. When he looked up, he was clean again.

He picked up the jar of minnows from the kitchen window sill. "Is this supper?"

Homer laughed, "No, Uncle. They are for Auntie to look at."

After a dinner of scrambled eggs, beans and sliced ham, Homer sat in the shade of the porch, his legs swinging over the edge. Uncle Lloyd came out and sat beside him. Homer felt him put his hand on his shoulder.

"It's very nice that you bring Auntie presents. Are you impatient about something?"

Homer looked up at his Uncle. "I can't wait for powwow, and I just want to see Lester so much."

Uncle smiled. "Since your mother and father passed away so long ago, you are now our son, as special to us as our own. Do you believe me?"

"Yes, Uncle," said Homer.

"You have the whole summer ahead of you. If you feel that impatient, before you know it will be over … so try to live one day at a time. Enjoy yourself, Homer. If you get ideas too big they might seem small when they happen. Be patient."

"I will try, but it's hard."

Homer looked out in the yard. His younger cousins, Ida and Darren, were chasing a little white and brown spotted dog in a circle. They were laughing and getting all dusty when they tripped over the puppy.

Uncle Lloyd called out, "Don't you hurt that little dog. Be careful!"

Just then a car came roaring down the road squealing to a stop. It was a long red convertible. The sun was setting behind it, making the people in it silhouettes. A figure jumped out of the back seat and stood straight against the sun. He grabbed a fat duffel bag and waved toward the house calling out, "Aho! Little brother!"

Homer squinted, then jumped up, "It's Lester!"

He ran off the porch, leaping right over his fallen bike until he reached his brother.

Lester was standing tall. He clicked his heels together, snapping up his hand in a salute. Homer thought he looked so important wearing a green uniform, with bright brass buttons, a wedge cap and shiny black shoes. Lester kept his hand up and said, "Is that what you do for a soldier?"

Homer tried to salute him back and Lester laughed, "No little brother, you give him a big hug!" And then Lester dropped down on one knee. Homer threw his arms around his neck.

"Auntie is making me moccasins for powwow!" blurted Homer.

Lester turned to the two other soldiers in the car. "See you in a couple weeks." Then the car made a fast U-turn and drove away.

Lester picked up his duffel bag and walked into the yard holding Homer's shoulder. Little Ida was squeezing the dog. "We got new puppies!" she said. Lloyd was waiting on the porch.

Homer ran up to his uncle, "Look, Lester has medals already!"

Lester smiled, "That's a sharpshooter's badge. See, Uncle, none of those other guys ever hunted squirrels. I was the best shot in my squad!"

"Big bragging," said Uncle Lloyd, "for a private!"

Before bedtime Lester opened his duffel bag. He rummaged around inside and brought out an envelope.

"They took pictures when we graduated." He handed one to his auntie and one to Homer. It was a color picture, with Lester standing in his dress uniform beside an American flag. He looked very serious.

Homer stared at the picture, the first he ever had of his brother. He turned it over and read: "For Homer, from your brother, Lester."

At bedtime, Homer and Lester went into the small back room with bunk beds. Homer put Lester's picture on a small table, standing it against a lamp as Lester took off his uniform.

"You can have the top bunk if you want, " said Homer. "But when you leave I want it back."

"In our barracks we had bunk beds, too, and I slept on top! Let's get some rest now," said Lester.

Lester turned off the lamp and climbed up top. Homer lay on the bottom bed thinking. After a few minutes he quietly asked, "Lester, where are you going?"

Lester turned in the bed. "Vietnam."

"Where's that?" asked Homer.

"Overseas … a long way from here."

The day before powwow, Auntie and a group of other women cooked huge amounts of food, soup and fry bread and meat. Homer finally tried on his new moccasins, which were beaded all in blue with red and yellow designs. Homer was bursting with pride as he practiced dancing, whirling in the front yard while his older brother sat on the edge of the porch, beating a drum and singing. The moccasins were a perfect fit—a little long so he could grow into them over the summer.

There was so much to do, and Homer helped out. In the afternoon Uncle Lloyd drove everyone to the powwow grounds, where the family had a campsite with a large wooden roof as a sunshade. Many families had campsites like these, and all during the powwow they fed any visitors who came by. The previous year

Homer's family fed a family from Germany. This afternoon, Homer and Lester carried out the wooden picnic tables and folding chairs, making sure everything would be ready for the next day's guests. It made Homer feel so warm inside to share their food with strangers, and he was always overwhelmed by all the people coming around, snapping pictures and shaking hands. There were so many wonderful things about powwow—the dancing and singing, the food, the new friends—that Homer couldn't decide which he liked best. Now the powwow arena was just an empty field, with wooden planks set on cinder blocks in a huge circle for the dancers to sit on. People were setting up the microphones in the center so everyone could hear the singers. Vendors were already arriving and covering their tables with bright blankets. By tomorrow there would be thousands of people, some from across the world! Homer sometimes thought the tourists were funny, but Auntie reminded him to have manners.

Time seemed to fly by for Homer. By bedtime he had everything ready. His new moccasins sat on the night table beside Lester's army picture, and his bustle—a bright, fan-shaped arrangement of colored feathers that he wore behind on his belt—was hanging from a nail on the wall. Lester had helped him shake it out and then use the steam from the spout of a kettle to fluff up the feathers. Homer had unfolded his special shirt of red calico, with blue and white satin ribbonwork, draping it over a chair. His roach, a long headpiece of porcupine guard hairs and deer tail hair, rested on a stand. One broad eagle feather stood up from the center to twirl and bob as he danced. When Homer went to bed, he lay in the darkness thinking about all the time and love it took to make a dance outfit—especially all the help he had, from Auntie, who made his moccasins, to Grannie who sewed his shirt. He had been told that it was impossible to ever dance alone, because the spirit of his family was always with him.

In the morning, Homer watched with pride as Lester polished his army shoes until they sparkled. Then Lester put on his uniform. There was something about it, Homer noticed, that made Lester stand taller. Lester helped Homer put on his dance outfit, working to get the bright red and white face paint just right.

Homer carried his bustle as he rode in the back of the pickup truck. Lester rode up front so he wouldn't get road dust all over his army uniform. As they approached the fairgrounds, it seemed to Homer that a whole city had grown up overnight. The fields were covered with row upon row of parked cars and pickups. The vendors were set up, and the smell of cooking hung in the air—fry bread, burgers, chili. The wooden bleachers beyond the dance arena were filling with spectators. The announcer was testing the microphone: "One—two—three … ."

Homer ran all over the fairgrounds, looking for his friends. He found Rick Crow, who was in his class at school and lived only a mile away.

"Good outfit!" said Homer, admiring Rick's new bustle of hawk feathers.

Rick looked down. "Nice shoes!" he said looking at Homer's moccasins.

Suddenly Homer tipped his ear listening to the public address loudspeakers.

"AHO, DANCERS. PLEASE, TAKE YOUR PLACES FOR GRAND ENTRY!"

"Let's go!" said Homer. The two boys rushed to the dance arena. There were hundreds of dancers. Some of the men were wearing old-time traditional outfits, some were wearing bright fancy dance outfits like Homer's. All the women were wearing shawls with long fringes that swayed when the women moved.

"Let's get up front!" said Homer as he ran with Rick to get right behind the flags.

Homer froze when he saw the flag bearers ready to enter the arena as the singing started up. There was Lester holding the American flag on a staff! Beside him stood a warrior in traditional regalia holding the Canadian flag. On either side of them was a dancer—one with the state flag of Oklahoma, and the other carrying the nation flag of the Native people.

"Rick look … my brother is carrying the flag!"

Homer pushed right up behind his brother and gave a quick tug on his uniform. Lester looked back. "Dance hard, little brother," he said smiling down at Homer.

Then a slow deep drum beat sounded in the air. Homer saw his brother's back straighten as he held up the flag. The announcer asked everyone to stand for grand entry, and the dancers began to move their feet against the earth in time to the drum. When the lead singer raised his voice and the second singer jumped in, Lester slowly led the dancers into the big arena.

Homer felt like his heart was flying as he kept in time with the drum, dancing amid the sharp sound of bells and hard drum beats. Slowly the procession of dancers, like a long snake, wound its way into the arena until they had all entered to stand in a huge circle around the center drum and the six singers.

The announcer reminded everyone to remain standing as a song was sung to honor all the veterans of all the wars. It was a slow song that Homer had heard many times. It was always sung to make people remember the soldiers who came home from war, those who had died in battle and those who had been wounded. Some of the dancers wore Purple Heart medals pinned to their outfits.

When the song was over the dancers cleared the arena, and Lester handed the flag to an old man wearing a faded uniform. The announcer called out, "We honor one of our own boys who is going overseas now. We thank him for his sacrifice. Please honor Private Lester John."

The drum started again. Homer's brother stood between the flag bearers, dancing alone in the arena. One by one, people came forward to shake Lester's hand; some of them put money in his hat, which he held upside down in front of him. Then they moved behind the flag bearers, continuing to dance as the train grew longer.

Homer ran out and shook his brother's hand, and Lester pulled him close, whispering, "Dance right up front with me." They circled the arena four times, and Homer never got tired.

Throughout the day Homer felt very strong. He danced thinking of his brother, and in between dances he ran to the campsite to eat good food and visit with relatives. Some of his family had traveled long distances to be there.

At the end of the day, Homer got a third-place ribbon in the junior fancy dancing category. Rick got a first place. Homer didn't care; he felt he was a big winner all day. He had been taught to be a good sport and thought it was great that Rick did so well dancing.

That night Homer had good thoughts. The sounds of the drum and the singer's voices were in his dreams.

Two days later the red convertible showed up early in the morning while Homer was still in bed.

Homer remembered his brother waking him before dawn to say good-bye, but he just wanted to dream about powwow.

Glossary

ALGONQUIN: A northeastern group of Native nations, from the Mic Mac to the Cree, Attikamek, Huron and many others, some of whom share similar languages.

APSAALOOKE: The original name of a northern Plains nation, often referred to as the Crow Tribe, presently located mostly in Montana. (Absoraka or Absoroka are commonly used spellings, although they are not the Crow spelling.)

ARENA: A place where people gather for dancing or sporting events, either indoors or outdoors, with a central open area for activities. Powwow arenas are always arranged in a circle, usually with the drum and singers in the middle, then ringed with dancers, then the spectators and lastly the booths for vendors.

BARRACKS: A building where military personnel live, work and sleep.

BEADWORK: An art form done by Native people. Small, colored "seed" beads are sewn onto leather or cloth in traditional or modern patterns, often with symbolic meaning to the artist.

BONJOUR: The French word for "Hello." French, not English, is a second language among many Native nations of the Northeast.

CHIRICAHUA: There are divisions or bands among the Apache nations, including the Chiricahua Apache, Jicarilla Apache, Mescalero Apache and White Mountain Apache.

CLAPBOARDED: A log house or home whose outside is covered with thin, overlapping boards.

COMMODITY: Dry goods or foods (including canned goods, flour, sugar, coffee and tea, raisins, etc.) distributed by the governments of Canada and the United States to Native people on reservations, often in fulfillment of treaty agreements.

CORN SOUP: A traditional soup of many Native people, especially in the Northeast, consisting of white corn kernels, kidney beans, and chunks of ham.

COULEE: A gully or natural ditch formed on the land after hundreds of years of rain eroding the earth. Smaller than a canyon.

CREE: A northern nation of people extending in a broad band across Canada.

CROW AGENCY: Named for the site of a government office that administered U.S. policies over the Apsaalooke people, located in southern Montana, near the Little Big Horn River.

DULCE: A town in northwestern New Mexico, which is the home and tribal offices of the Jicarilla Apache nation.

FANCY DANCE: A fast traditional dance at powwows. The male dancers wear bright feather objects on the back waist and back neck called bustles—often dyed a rainbow of colors. The bustles shake and bounce with the dancer's movements. Women fancy dancers usually wear bright shawls with long fringe, which spin like bird wings as they dance to the fast beat of the men singing on the big drum.

FRY BREAD: A traditional food developed by Native people after the Europeans brought wheat flour to America. A thick dough is made and fried in hot grease or oil to make big round fluffy bread, often folded with chili inside to make "Indian tacos."

GERONIMO: A Chiricahua Apache leader who is as important to Native people as many American leaders are to non-Native Americans. Native American children grow up learning the stories of many Native role-models— Cornplanter, Handsome Lake, Medicine Crow, Manuelito, Sitting Bull, Gall, Red Jacket, Thayendenegea, Chief Joseph, Almighty Voice, Crazy Horse, Louis Riel, just the same way other American children learn about George Washington, Benjamin Franklin and Thomas Jefferson within their culture.

GUNWALES: The top outside edge of a canoe or boat. Pronounced "gun-ells."

HULL: The outside shape or covering of a boat or canoe.

J-STROKE: A way to pull a paddle through the water that makes the canoe turn in an opposite direction.

JICARILLA: An Apache nation.

KEEL: A long narrow strip of wood along the bottom length of a canoe that helps the canoe to travel in a straight line. Birchbark canoes do not have a keel, so the paddler must control the direction of the canoe with different kinds of paddling/stroke techniques.

KOYUKON: A nation of inland Alaska Native people who hunt, trap and fish to maintain traditional and ancient ways of survival and lifestyle. The Koyukon use modern ways now, such as snowmobiles and chainsaws, but continue to respect the environment.

LACROSS(E): Called the Creator's Game by the Hotinoshonni (Iroquois), lacrosse is a contest of teams to catch and throw a ball using sticks curved at the end with a small net made of rawhide thongs. Other nations play a similar game, such as the Creek of Oklahoma, who call it stickball. Although it is a rough fast game like hockey, it is rooted in spiritual values and was sometimes used to settle disputes among villages.

MOCCASINS: Indian shoes. There are many kinds, depending on the nation, and the commercial types sold by large companies are not authentic Indian moccasins.

MOHAWK: A nation of northeast people who called themselves Kanien:keha'ka—"People of the place of Flint." The Mohawk are part of a confederacy called Hotinoshonni (People of the Longhouse), also called "Iroquois" by the French, or "Six Nations" by the English. The other members are the Oneida, Onondaga, Cayuga, Seneca and Tuscorora.

OTTAWA: The capital of Canada, but also the name of that region's people, properly called Odawa.

PICTOGRAPHIC: Art, either in beadwork, quillwork or paint, that looks like pictures of people, animals or plants.

PURPLE HEART: An award created by George Washington during the American Revolutionary War to honor soldiers who made great sacrifices. Now it is a medal given to all American military people who have been wounded while serving their country. More percentages of Native Americans join the military than any other ethnic group, and those Indians who have been wounded sometimes wear their Purple Heart medals on their traditional dance outfits at powwows.

QUILLWORK: Unique to North America, the white quills of the porcupine are dyed various colors with vegetable or chemical (modern) dyes and are used in a variety of decorative applied art forms, especially embroidery.

RAVEN: A large black corvine bird, resembling a crow.

RAWHIDE: Untanned hide or skin of buffalo, elk, moose or deer, which is hard and stiff, and often used for moccasin soles, painted containers called parfleche or drum heads.

REGALIA: The term for traditional or contemporary Native American dance outfits, clothing and accessories.

RIBBON SHIRT: A shirt made of satin or flowered calico cloth with strips of bright ribbon sewn on, often left to dangle on the ends, and worn at powwows or other traditional gatherings.

RIBBONWORK: Using wide satin ribbons cut in floral or geometric designs to embroider on women's shawls, leggings, skirts and dresses.

ROAN: A horse with a red or brown base of hair peppered with scattered white hairs.

SAC and **FOX:** A nation of Native people originally from the Michigan area, now scattered in parts of Iowa and Oklahoma, whose indigenous name is Mesquakie, meaning the "Red Earths."

SHEATH: A case for a knife.

SKINNER: The person who removes the hide from a deer or moose or other animal during the butchering process.

SNOWMOBILE: Also called snow machine, it is a treaded vehicle for traveling in snow in northern regions.

SUNSHADE: A circular arbor of tree branches around a powwow arena to shade the spectators from the sun.

TIPI: Conical "tents" used for dwellings by the Plains nations. The word tipi comes from the Lakota language, meaning "to dwell in."

TRICKSTER: A person or creature, often the Coyote, of Native stories, who is a troublemaker or prankster, but often in comical ways.

WATER DRUM: A small wooden drum with a leather head, which is partially filled with water to change its pitch when tapped with a tiny wooden carved beater stick.